Published by Hachette Partworks Ltd.
ISBN: 978-1-908648-74-7
Date of Printing: August 2013
Printed in Malaysia by Tien Wah Press

TinkerBell
and the
SECRET
of the
WINGS

Disney
Hachette

There was once a land called Pixie Hollow. It was a magical place, where all four seasons existed, side by side, throughout the year.

One day, Tinker Bell was helping her friend Fawn to move the animals to their home for the winter. Tink wished that she could visit the Winter Woods too!

"But you know we can never go there," Fawn reminded Tink.

There was a rule that warm fairies were not allowed over the border to the Winter Woods, and winter fairies couldn't cross the other way.

But as soon as Fawn wasn't looking, Tinker
Bell sneaked onto the bridge between the two
seasons and crossed over.

What a magical sight! Tink was so
captivated that she forgot all about
the cold – and that she wasn't supposed
to be there.

Suddenly, Tink noticed that her wings had
begun to sparkle.

Just then, Fawn lassoed Tink and yanked her back over the border. The strange shimmering stopped, but Tinker Bell couldn't stop thinking about it.

At the library, Tink found a
book all about wingology –
but the bookworm had chewed the page on
sparkling wings!
The Reading Fairy told her that the only
person who could help her was the Keeper,
who lived in the Winter Woods.

The next day, Tink put on the warm coat she had made. The coat covered her wings, so she needed to hitch a ride. She sneaked into a basket of snowflakes, which was soon picked up by an owl on his way to the Winter Woods.

After a while, Tink landed with a bump – on a frozen lake. She had arrived!

Tinker Bell made her way to the Winter
Library, where she found the Keeper, whose name
was Dewey, working at his desk.

But before Tink could speak to him, another
fairy appeared – and her wings were sparkling,
just like Tink's!

When Dewey saw the
two fairies, he understood
at once.

He explained that
their wings shimmered
whenever they were near
each other because they
were sisters!

Everybody knows that fairies are born when a baby laughs. Tinker Bell and the other fairy, Periwinkle, had been born from the same laugh, which had split in two as soon as it left the baby's mouth.

Dewey said that Tink had to go
home straight away, but the fairies
were so thrilled to meet each other
that he agreed to let them spend a
little time together.

They had a wonderful afternoon! Tink couldn't bear to think she wouldn't see her new sister again, so she thought of a plan. Before she left, Tink whispered instructions to Periwinkle.

The next day, Periwinkle arrived
at the bridge. She and her friends
were carrying a huge block of ice.
Tink was already waiting there,
with Bobble and Clank – and a
large, very strange-looking machine!

It was a snow machine. Now Periwinkle would be able to stay cool on her visit to the Warm Side!

When Rosetta gave Periwinkle
a flower, she gave it a coating of
shimmering frost.

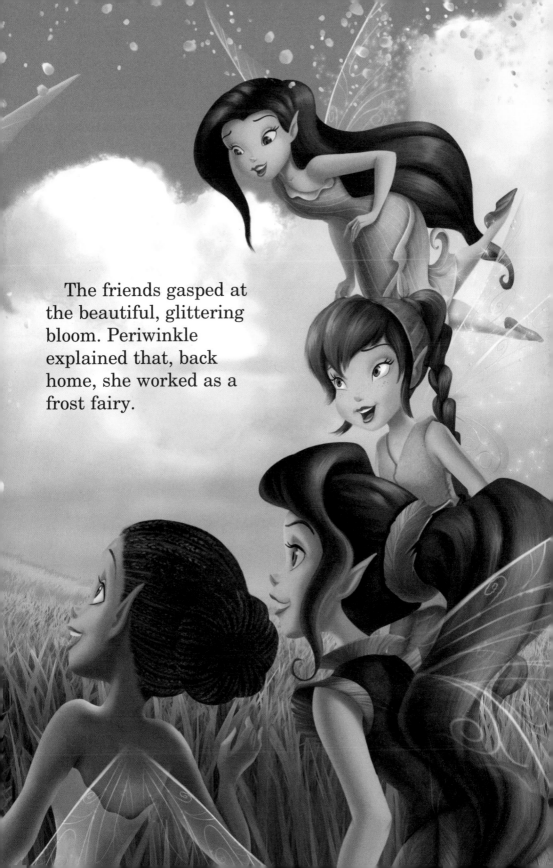

The friends gasped at the beautiful, glittering bloom. Periwinkle explained that, back home, she worked as a frost fairy.

But after a while, Periwinkle began to feel a little faint.

The snow machine was running out of ice and Periwinkle's wings were wilting fast!

The fairies rushed Periwinkle back
to the border, where Milori, Lord of the
Winter Woods, was waiting.

"This is why we do not cross the
border," he said angrily. "The rule is
there to protect you!"

The sisters
hugged, knowing
they might never
see each other
again.

As he flew off, Lord Milori pushed the snow machine into the frozen river.

That night, Queen Clarion and Lord Milori each
told the same story to the young fairies.

"Long ago, when Pixie Hollow was very young, a winter fairy and a fairy from the Warm Seasons met and fell in love.

"Their love grew so strong that they disregarded the danger. One of them crossed the border and broke a wing, for which there is no cure. The two fairies had to say goodbye.

"From that day, it was decreed that fairies must never again cross the border. The two worlds had to remain apart forever."

As Queen Clarion finished her story, Tinker Bell noticed something strange. It was snowing!

The Queen and the fairies flew to see what was going on. All of a sudden, a huge whirlwind loomed in front of them.

"Let's not panic," said the Queen reassuringly.

Tink flew to investigate.
The snow machine was stuck
on the frozen river, churning
out a tornado of snowflakes.
    The fairies tried with
all their might to free the
trapped machine.

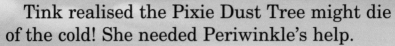

Tink realised the Pixie Dust Tree might die of the cold! She needed Periwinkle's help.

Tink flew to the Winter Woods and showed Periwinkle the frosted flower, which was still alive and as lovely as ever.

"The frost acts like a blanket. It traps the warm air inside and keeps out the cold," explained one of the frost fairies.

"We could frost the Pixie Dust Tree before the freeze hits it!" cried Periwinkle.

The frost fairies got to work straight away. They sprinkled frost all over the land, putting a double coating on the magic tree.

The plan worked. When the sun came out and thawed the tree, the pixie dust began to flow again.

The valley was safe!

But just then, Periwinkle noticed Tink's wing. It was damaged! The two sisters hugged each other sadly… and then something wonderful happened. Their wings sparkled and shimmered together until Tink's broken wing was magically healed.

From then on, warm fairies could visit winter fairies whenever they liked – as long as they frosted their wings first, to protect them from the cold.

And it wasn't only Tink and Periwinkle who were thrilled that they could be together again – so were Queen Clarion and Lord Milori!